A NEAR THING FOR CAPTAIN NAJORK

Russell Hoban

&

Quentin Blake

WALKER BOOKS

AND SUBSIDIARIES

LONDON · BOSTON · SYDNEY · AUCKLAND

First published 1975 by Jonathan Cape Ltd ✦ Published 2014 by Walker Books Ltd, 87 Vauxhall Walk, London SE11 5HJ ✦ This edition published 2015 ✦ Text © 1975 the Estate of Russell Hoban ✦ Illustrations © 1975 Quentin Blake ✦ The right of Russell Hoban and Quentin Blake to be identified as author and illustrator respectively of this work has been asserted by them in accordance with the Copyright, Designs and Patents Act 1988 ✦ This book has been typeset in Goudy Old Style ✦ Printed in China ✦ All rights reserved ✦ No part of this book may be reproduced, transmitted or stored in an information retrieval system in any form or by any means, graphic, electronic or mechanical, including photocopying, taping and recording, without prior written permission from the publisher. ✦ British Library Cataloguing in Publication Data: a catalogue record for this book is available from the British Library ✦ ISBN 978-1-4063-5564-2 ✦ www.walker.co.uk ✦ 10 9 8 7 6 5 4 3 2 1

One morning after breakfast Tom was fooling around with his chemistry set and he invented anti-sticky.

Then he fooled around with anti-sticky and jam and springs
and wheels and connecting-rods and he made a two-seater
jam-powered frog.

Tom got into the frog with Aunt Bundlejoy Cosysweet and
started it up. The frog hopped over the fence and the next
three gardens in one giant hop.

"What makes it go?" said Aunt Bundlejoy.

"Jam," said Tom. "When the anti-sticky plate hits the sticky it bounces back. The spring keeps it going, the connecting-rods move up and down, the wheels go round and the frog hops."

Tom and Aunt Bundlejoy took the frog out for a spin.

Captain Najork was in the observatory looking through his telescope at the girls' boarding-school across the river when the frog hopped past. "Follow that frog!" he shouted to his hired sportsmen as he hopped into his pedal-powered snake, and away they undulated.

Captain Najork had not forgotten the time when Tom had beaten him and his sportsmen at womble, muck and sneedball. "I'd like to try some new games on him," said the Captain. "I'd like to see how good he is at thud, crunch and Tom-on-the-bottom."

Aunt Fidget Wonkham-Strong Najork
came up the observatory stairs singing
"Heart of Oak". She had tea and scones
for the Captain's elevenses – but he was
not there.

She looked out of the window and
saw that the Captain's snake was gone.

She looked through the telescope
and saw the Headmistress of the girls'
boarding-school practising two-handed
clean-and-jerks with her bar-bells.
"Aha!" said Aunt Fidget Wonkham-
Strong Najork.

She put on her flippers and snorkel, swam across the river
and knocked at the girls' boarding-school door.

"Can I help you, madam?" said the caretaker.

Aunt Fidget Wonkham-Strong Najork knocked him down
and went straight to the Headmistress's office.

"Where is the Captain?" she said.

"Of which team?" said the Headmistress. "Hockey, squash or lacrosse?"

"You know whom I mean," said Aunt Fidget Wonkham-Strong Najork. "Produce him instantly."

"You're dripping on my carpet," said the Headmistress.

"Very well," said Aunt Fidget Wonkham-Strong Najork. "I will arm-wrestle you for Captain Najork. Best out of three."

Meanwhile …

Tom and Aunt Bundlejoy hopped on in the jam-powered frog.

"We're being followed by a five-seater snake," said Aunt Bundlejoy.

"That must be Captain Najork," said Tom. "Does he want to race?"

"I think he wants to swallow us," said Aunt Bundlejoy. "The snake has got its mouth wide open."

"Bad luck," said Tom. "We're running out of sticky and I've left the jam at home."

"They're bound to have pots of jam at the girls' boarding-school," said Aunt Bundlejoy.

Tom turned the frog round, and away
they went back up the river with the
snake only a few frog-lengths behind.

"You beat us at womble!" shouted
the Captain. "You beat us at muck and
sneedball! But you won't win this time!"

Tom and Aunt Bundlejoy barely cleared the boarding-school wall
with the frog's last hop.

Aunt Bundlejoy knocked on the door.

"Can I help you, madam?" said the caretaker.

"Our frog's out of jam," said Aunt Bundlejoy. "Can you lend us a pot?"

"Just a moment, please," said the caretaker. "I'll have to ask the Headmistress for the keys to the jam locker."

As the caretaker came into the Headmistress's office, he saw the head of Captain Najork's snake at the open window. "There is a lady at the door who wants a pot of jam and there is a snake at the window, madam," he said.

"I can't be interrupted now," said the Headmistress. "Ask them to wait."

When Aunt Fidget Wonkham-Strong Najork saw the snake, she was so cross with the Captain that she flung the Headmistress through the window into the snake's open mouth.

"Oy!" said the Captain. He stepped on the ejector-pedal
and the Headmistress shot back through the window and flattened
Aunt Fidget Wonkham-Strong Najork. As his wife's feet flew up,
Captain Najork recognized her flippers.

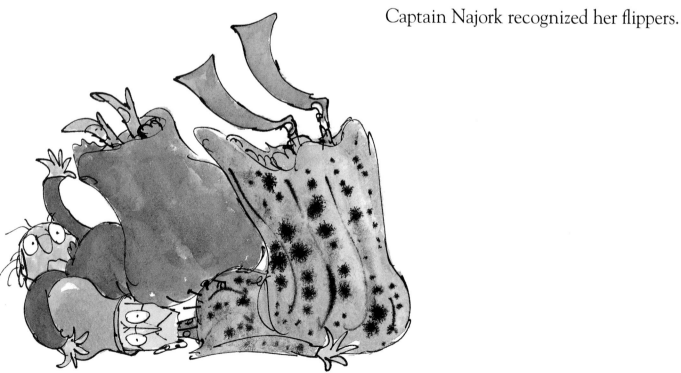

"May I have my wife, please?" he said to the caretaker.

The caretaker handed Aunt Fidget Wonkham-Strong Najork out to the Captain and he put her on a sofa in the snake's lounge.

"I think we had better go home now," he said to the hired sportsmen, and they undulated back over the wall and away.

Now that she'd seen Captain Najork, the Headmistress had taken a fancy to him. "After them!" she shouted to Tom and Aunt Bundlejoy. "We haven't finished arm-wrestling!"

"We're out of jam," said Tom.

A pot of jam was quickly fetched and they hopped off after the snake.

They caught up with it at the landing-stage by Aunt Fidget Wonkham-Strong Najork's house.

As the Captain was helping his wife ashore, the Headmistress leapt out of the frog and plucked at Aunt Fidget Wonkham-Strong Najork's sleeve.

"That's quite all right," said Aunt Fidget Wonkham-Strong Najork. "No explanations are necessary. The Captain has convinced me that my suspicions were unfounded."

"Never mind that," said the Headmistress. "You said best out of three and we haven't even finished one."

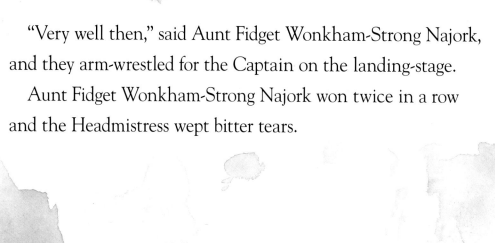

"Very well then," said Aunt Fidget Wonkham-Strong Najork,
and they arm-wrestled for the Captain on the landing-stage.
Aunt Fidget Wonkham-Strong Najork won twice in a row
and the Headmistress wept bitter tears.

"The Captain would have lent such an air to the establishment!" she said.

"Did you want to play some more games?" said Tom to the Captain.

"He can't," said Aunt Fidget Wonkham-Strong Najork. "He's got to have his lunch and he'll be learning off pages of the Nautical Almanac for the rest of the day."

"Eat your swede-and-mutton slump," said Aunt Fidget Wonkham-Strong Najork to the Captain. "And think how lucky you are to be here. That was a near thing for you today."

"Yes, dear," said the Captain. He ate it.